THE LAST CASE

A WILKINSON'S DETECTIVE AGENCY SHORT STORY

ALEXANDRIA BLAELOCK

Also by Alexandria Blaelock

SHORT STORY COLLECTIONS
The Haunting of Hayward Hall
Lovelorn, Lovestruck and Love at First Sight
Common or Garden Variety Heroes
Case Files of the Wilkinson Detective Agency
Unavoidable Fates
Christmas Travesties
Five Faces of Felicia Clarke

FICTION
That Love Nonsense
Taipan vs Brown

MS BLAELOCK'S BOOKS
Stress Free Dinner Parties
Signature Wardrobe Planning
Holistic Personal Finance
Minimally Viable Housekeeping
Planning a Life Worth Living

A SELECTION OF AVAILABLE SHORT STORIES
Alma'that thas Grace
Fate in Your Hands
Kiss of Death
Lady of the Looking Glass
Life in the Security Directorate
Morning Star, Evening Star, Superstar
Payton's Run
Secret Singer
Shining Star
Ship in a Bottle
Simone Says Hands in the Air
The Day the Schedule Broke

THE LAST CASE

A WILKSINSON'S DETECTIVE
AGENCY SHORT STORY

ALEXANDRIA BLAELOCK

BlueMere Books
MELBOURNE, AUSTRALIA

For permission requests, please contact
enquiries@bluemerebooks.com.

Ordering Information:
Discounts are available on quantity purchases. For details, contact orders@bluemerebooks.com.

The Last Case/Alexandria Blaelock
paperback ISBN: 978-1-922744-61-6
digital ISBN: 978-1-922744-62-3

Book Layout © BookDesignTemplates.com
Cover Art © Vadim Guzhva/depositphotos

THE LAST CASE

It was the kind of beautiful, crisp, clear winter's day that Lily White loved. She walked down the grass verge beside the path, enjoying the crunching of frost beneath her boots, and as she turned the corner, the sight of a single set of footprints descending the hill.

She loved snuggling into her hat and scarf, the cold biting at the tops of her cheeks as she started walking.

And she loved unravelling the scarf and opening her bright blue overcoat as she got to the bottom of the hill and warmed up.

Then wrapping herself up again as she waited at the train station, and unravelling as the carriage filled up with passengers and the temperature rose.

But most of all, she loved watching the hot air balloons, suspended in the cloudless sky above Melbourne as her train approached the city.

As was her custom, she ordered a latte at the café downstairs, checked the mailbox, and bounded up the three flights of stairs rather than waiting for the ancient lift.

The Nicholas Building was completed in 1926; the stairs wound tightly around the lift well and were the perfect height for comfortably climbing. Even for someone as petite as Lily.

As she reached her floor, she paused to admire the varnished red wood solidity of her door, as she pulled the key from her pocket and turned it in the old, worn, brass deadlock.

"I'm here Gramps," she called as she opened the door.

He didn't answer, but that wasn't really a surprise. He'd been out on a surveillance job the night before and might have stopped off to freshen up and take a nap on the way in.

She put the mail on her desk, noticed the answering machine wasn't flashing messages waiting to be heard, then took a sip of coffee and turned the ancient heater on.

Lily was just warm enough from the run up the stairs to take her outer layers off, knowing the heater would have warmed up by the point she was about ready to put them back on again.

The down side of an older building was the old black steel crittal window frames. They looked beautiful but had absolutely no thermal properties.

Not to worry, Gramps said she was a softy just like all young people today. He himself was of an age where he thought fresh air was more important than heat and always kept the windows a tiny bit open.

And they did look lovely set against the white walls, so perhaps in this instance, form trumped function.

The office was decorated with what passed for Sherlock Holmes-style furniture in the 1940s.

As you walked in the door, to your right was her desk, a non-adjustable real wood desk with one big drawer under the main writing surface, and smaller drawers down the right-hand side that meant she had to use a footstool and a cushion on the chair to reach a comfortable height.

She'd always meant to get a proper ergonomic chair, but as tiny as she was, she'd almost certainly need a custom make. The idea of a childsize office desk and chair was more than she could cope with.

Next to the desk, between the wall and the desk, was a low, lateral filing cabinet that held their archived cases. She used its top for her trays and the phone.

On the other side, the waiting room consisted of a slim, wood-framed burgundy upholstered lounge suite of coffee table, two armchairs and a sofa.

When Gran insisted on upgrading their household furniture, it had been sent to the office.

Gramps sometimes napped on the couch though he was too tall to rest up comfortably.

The magazines were only a decade or so out of date.

On a normal day, she liked to dress a little bit retro, in keeping with the era. Nothing obvious, just heels, a pencil skirt and blouse.

The room smelled of Gramps' cigars, and very faintly of the beeswax and lavender furniture polish Gran used to use.

Even when building management forbade smoking in the building, he opened the windows and leant on the wall, looking down on the street to enjoy his cigar and whisky at the end of the day.

Overall, the office looked like a film set, with the morning sun shining through the wood and mottled glass wall dividing the front from Gramps at the back. Highlighting the letters painstakingly painted onto the door with a golden glow that was only half in her imagination.

Lewis White

Private Investigator

According to Gran, it was his colleagues at the Wilkinson National Detective Agency who'd paid to have the sign on the door when he'd left.

She took another sip of coffee, and pulled her laptop out of the filing cabinet, opening it and turning it on before taking the day's newspaper back to put on his desk.

She opened the partition door and was shocked into stillness at the condition of the room.

It was an utter shambles; furniture overturned, papers fanned out across the floor, and even odder, Gramps' jacket and hat, still on the overturned hat rack.

There was no way he'd left the office in that condition.

She shut the door, retreated to her desk, and called the Police.

Not too much later, a young constable arrived to take stock of the scene. He was cute if you liked big blond-haired, blue-eyed guys.

Which Lily did.

"Constable Declan Gill," he introduced himself.

"Private Investigator Lily White," she said offering her hand.

Constable Gill took out his notebook, "what seems to be the trouble here."

Lily opened the door, and indicated the mess inside, "we've been burgled; this room was as neat as the other when I left last night."

The constable looked from the messy room to the tidy room. "What was taken?"

"I haven't had a chance to look. I thought you'd need to get the crime scene guys in before I checked or something."

A smile chased across his face and was gone almost before she noticed, "do you have any cameras here in the office, or on this floor?"

"Aaahh. No. I think there might be some in the elevators and on the ground floor to protect the stained-glass ceilings, but not up here."

"I see, and did you see anyone when you left last night?"

"The tenants on this side were gone, but I think there might have been someone on the other side, I could see a light. I didn't see any people waiting around though."

He stood in the doorway, looking around the room, "no footprints, no obvious contaminants." He pulled a little fingerprint kit from a pocket in his utility vest and stepped through the door to dust a few test surfaces including the sides of the bookshelves and desk.

"Whoever did this was likely wearing gloves," he turned to look at her, "I'll take the report back, but I have to be honest with you. If you can't tell me exactly what was taken, and even if you do, it's unlikely anything further will come of this report."

If Lily was honest, she was annoyed with how offhand the constable was.

And once he'd gone, and she looked through the door at the mess again, she realised he had a point.

She had no idea whether anything was missing.

And no idea where to start looking for it. Starting seemed more problematic than finishing.

Perhaps if she started putting things back in order, she'd be better able to tell what was missing.

But she'd need some more appropriate clothes for moving the furniture, and luckily, she'd forgotten to take her gym clothes home. Several times...

After a quick trip to the lady's toilet downstairs, she was ready to wade into the mess of Gramps' office.

First, she closed the laptop and stacked it with the mail and phone on top of the trays, which she stacked one on top of the other. She picked up the hat rack and carried it behind her desk next to the filing cabinet, smoothing Gramps' jacket down and carefully placing his hat on the top.

Then she started picking up the books, papers and ornaments, randomly stacking them on and around her desk and the filing cabinet. Followed by the chairs and coffee table as well.

When the floor was mostly clear, it was time to start righting the furniture.

At which point, it became clear what the limitations of her 148 cm frame were.

She saw Gramps' half-full whisky bottle in the corner. Perhaps a tot of whisky might give her the strength she needed.

She'd just taken a swig from the bottle, and was appreciating the burn in her throat, (which overlaid the desire to cry tears of frustration) when someone cleared their throat behind her.

As she swung around, she hid the bottle and lid behind her back.

It was the young constable again, taking in the changes the last couple of hours had made.

Kind enough to ignore the whisky, though he must have seen it.

"Er, you might need another of those Miss White."

She brazened it out, putting the stopper on the whisky and easing it onto the corner of her desk, "you couldn't give me a hand with this," she stuck her thumb over her right shoulder to indicate the office, "could you?"

"Urm, we're really not supposed to...

"Sure, why not."

He walked into the room and took hold of a bookshelf, "just back against the wall?"

"Yes," she said, following him in.

He heaved the shelf up.

"Careful," she said, as books that had previously been held in by the leg of the desk cascaded down.

She hesitated for a moment before sweeping them out of the way with a foot and moving to help with the next bookshelf and then the last.

Drawers had spilled out of the desk, so they stacked them in a corner before setting that right.

Then emptying Gramps' old filing cabinets because it was easier to lift them that way.

"Does anything look to be missing?" he asked.

Lily sighed and wiped a smear of dust across her forehead, "Now you ask?" she looked around, "I can't really tell without putting it all back."

"Come sit down," he said, pulling her into the waiting room and moving a stack of papers from one of the armchairs to the floor nearby, "there's something I need to tell you."

And moving a stack from the other so he could drag it closer to her.

She got up to pull a bottle of water from her bag and take a drink.

Constable Gill took a deep breath, "I have some bad news for you," he looked into her face, gauging her reaction.

"This morning we were called to a scene in Essendon where we found Mr Lewis, deceased, in his car. The coroner believes the cause of death may have been a heart attack."

The colour drained from Lily's face, and Declan caught the water bottle as she lifted her hands to her face.

"The death is not considered suspicious at this stage," he said screwing the lid back on, "but I have to ask you whether you know what he was doing in Essendon."

Lily scrubbed her face with her hands, and took a deep breath, "I'll need to check the computer."

She climbed to her feet, and almost slid over a stack of papers. He leapt to his feet and pushed her back into the chair, "I'll go."

He brought her laptop over, opening the lid for her.

She crossed her legs on the armchair and typed her password to gain entry to the system, but there was nothing there.

No programmes.

No files.

Absolutely nothing there.

She checked the recycle bin on the landing page, and that was empty too.

She slapped the keys with both hands in frustration, and still nothing.

She turned it over, looking at the case. It appeared to be her laptop, with the ancient cute puppy sticker still affixed, though that didn't mean that the innards hadn't been replaced.

"It's empty," she said stupidly.

"May I look?" he asked.

She handed it over, "why would someone do that? I can't imagine anyone on the kind of domestic scale we specialise in making that much effort."

"Oh, people can get—"

"Wouldn't they rather throw the goddammed thing on the floor and hit it with a baseball bat a couple of times.?"

"It seems more deliberate than that—"

"But his office was just trashed... Maybe they were angry when they couldn't find whatever it was on the one and only computer in the office."

"Then it's gone forever, and we won't know for sure why."

Lily cackled like a witch, and Declan looked at her sharply.

"No it isn't, I have a backup. I take a backup every day; one in the cloud and one on an external drive I take away with me."

"You do what?"

"Yes," she grinned, "there was an incident with faulty wiring a few years ago and we lost everything. I wasn't taking that chance again. It took forever to recreate the files."

"Then I'll just take the drive back to the office."

And that was it, back on the case - Lily would let herself grieve later.

"No you won't. Not without a warrant. I need the details on the backup to reconstruct the cases."

"Surely you can let it go and let the Police take over now."

"No, I can't. I have responsibilities to our clients; they've paid good money to resolve the issues that matter to them."

"Aren't you just the receptionist?"

She laughed, a genuine laugh, as though he'd told a great joke.

"Is that what you think? That's too precious." She snapped the laptop shut and walked to the desk, clearing a space to lay it down, hardly bothered that half the papers she'd laboriously stacked it with earlier fell on the floor.

"But I thought..."

"We're actually the White Family Investigations." She rifled through her handbag until she found her wallet, and pulled a card from it, "I told you before, Private Investigator," and flicked him her license.

"I do the online stuff," she said, connecting her external drive, "and Gramps does the real world."

He didn't correct her on the tense.

"Before he died," she started typing, "Dad did the computer stuff until I came on board. Mum and Gran were the receptionists in the old days, but they're both gone now too."

He handed her back the card, "so what's next?"

She paused, waiting for the laptop to access the drive's data, "well, I'll close out the old cases, and probably move the business closer to home. Or at least I will when I get my Private Security Business Licence," she said smiling at him.

She started typing again.

"Now, let's see. He was working on a couple of things...

"Lost dog in Heidelberg, art theft in Moonee Ponds, missing person in Northcote, so nothing that close to Essendon."

She ran her hands through her hair, "this would be so much easier if I had his daybook. It's where he notes all the information about his day

- who he's spoken to, what cases he takes, and so on. I'd be able to check where he was up to on his current cases, and why he was in Essendon last night."

She paused to look at him, "unless he just stopped for a bit of shopping?"

He shook his head slightly, "even if it's in his car, it will be held as evidence until we can confirm the cause of death."

She frowned at him, "even if you do, you won't be able to read it. It's in code, and I'd appreciate it back as soon as possible."

She typed for a moment more, then stopped to look at him, "is there anything else you need?"

"What? Oh. No. There's nothing else Policewise, though you may need to come down to the station to make a statement. The office, and laptop drive, in conjunction with the deceased, make a suspicious series of events."

"Well," she said, "don't let me keep you from your investigations, I can manage the rest on my own."

"Are you sure?"

"Of course, you've done the hard stuff."

He took a step back from the desk, "all right. But you'll let me know when you find out if anything's missing?"

"Of course."

He walked to the door, and paused before passing through it, "may I call in tomorrow to see how you're getting on?"

She smiled, "of course. I'd like that."

She watched him leave, and waited a minute or two more, before allowing herself a moment or two to stand by the window, allowing her eyes to blur over.

Gramps was dead, and she was all alone in the world.

And then she pulled herself together. Pulling her track pants up and redoing the ties before pulling her t-shirt down.

She had three cases to look into, not to mention getting to the bottom of Gramps' death.

Then she could let herself fall into grief.

But first, lunch.

Somewhere else.

She locked the office, walked down the stairs, and out into the street, trotting down a nearby alleyway until she came to a small food court where she ordered a big bowl of noodles and a small glass of wine.

Pulling out her daybook, she tried to make sense of the day.

Hard drive wiped

Office trashed

G dead at Essendon

Cases Heidelberg, Moonee Ponds, Northcote

Dog, painting, missing person

What she hadn't mentioned to Declan, was that the missing person was a personal case.

Someone Gramps had lost contact with when he'd fallen in with a bad crowd.

Someone Gramps had been fairly sure had been murdered.

Not that it mattered, she hadn't been lying when she said she needed his daybook to see where he was up to.

In the meantime, there was still the matter of finding out if anything else had been stolen from the office. She finished up her lunch and left.

When she got back to the office, she started by checking all the surfaces of the desk and bookshelves; inspired by old detective shows where the thing you were looking for was taped underneath the desk, but not finding anything.

So much for that then.

When she got all the books back on the shelves, she discovered some of them were missing. And with all the ornaments and souvenirs back in place, there were a few pieces not accounted for when she'd pieced together enough of the fragments to see what was there.

She'd almost cried over the remains of the "World's Best Detective" mug that came from his Wilkinson's colleagues as well.

But with the office more or less in order once again, it looked weirdly empty without Gramps in it.

There were still the stacks of paper to go through, but by that point, she was exhausted. Reorganising the office had been the last thing on her mind when she arrived that morning.

She didn't even bother to get changed, just threw on her overcoat and went home.

She spent more of the night awake than asleep, and in the end, got up early and caught the train back into town.

Dressed more practically in jeans, sneakers and a thick fleece jacket.

She was on the way so early, the train never really filled up, and there was next to no one about.

Even her café hadn't opened its doors - they told her to come back in half an hour when the espresso machine had warmed up.

She stood in the doorway, trying to see and feel whether anything was different. Or what it was that had prevented her from settling.

There was just the usual, with papers stacked all over the desk and chairs and the floor.

And then it hit her - she hadn't checked her desk.

Someone had to have got into her filing cabinet to get at the laptop. And maybe they'd started with the desk.

She smoothed a hand down the sides of her drawers to discover someone had jimmied the lock, which was a bit funny because she'd never locked it. The wood had warped and it was all about the technique of pulling them out.

She pulled all the drawers out and felt around in the cavities.

Something had been taped to the underside of the desk, so she pulled it out, unwrapped it to find a thumb drive.

She left it aside for the moment, and checked all the sides of the drawers, taking a quick look to see that nothing appeared to be missing, (and discovering a few items she thought had been lost).

She took her laptop out of the filing cabinet and plugged the thumb drive into it, giving it a moment to connect while she flicked through the folders to see if anything was missing.

It looked fine, but she wasn't actually confident she could remember everything that was in there.

She'd been planning to send a bunch of stuff to their archival storage but hadn't quite got a box full.

And wasn't real keen on paying to send and store one that wasn't.

The laptop made the kind of whirl that indicated it had connected to the drive, so she opened it up to find a load of photographs, dated a couple of weeks ago.

She opened one at random, and it showed two men fighting in some kind of alleyway at night. She opened another to see the two again, only the lighting and focus was slightly better, and the man on the left was looking a bit worse for wear.

And another where the only reason he was upright, was because the other man was holding his shirt, his arm drawn back to punch him.

In the next, he was slumped on the ground, and the other walking away, turning his head backwards to spit.

She wasn't entirely sure what she was seeing, so she went back to the first in the series and flicked through them one at a time to show what was beginning to look like a murder.

She looked around the office, suddenly feeling cold, and realising she hadn't turned the heater on.

But still feeling she was being watched.

She pulled the drive from the laptop and slipped it into her jacket pocket.

She was just locking the door again when she heard the lift clanking as it approached the floor and came to a stop.

She raced down the corridor and around the corner so whoever was coming up didn't see her.

And when she heard to door to the lift well close, back around to the other side to run down the stairs.

In case there was a lookout, she went through the café, and ducked out the street entrance.

She ran the two city blocks to the East Melbourne police station, not daring to look back for signs of pursuit; hoping it was Declan's station, and he would be there.

She bent over just inside the door gasping for air, trying to see down the street.

"Can I help you Ma'am?"

She turned to see a female officer at the reception counter, "Ma'am?"

"Declan," she gasped, trying to get her breathing back under control, "Constable Declan Gill."

"One moment," she said, walking through a door separating the back office from the front reception counter.

After a few seconds, she was more or less under control and took a seat to wait. Swinging her legs a little as she waited.

And after a short eternity, he came to meet her.

Wordlessly she held out the drive to him.

He nodded, "would you come with me please?"

He put her in a small room, "coffee?"

She nodded, and he left her for a few moments before returning with a small, milky, sugary vending machine cup.

She looked at him doubtfully.

"It's not the best, but it's what we have," he said, "wait here and I'll see the detective."

Another short eternity and he arrived with a detective carrying a laptop and a file.

"Detective Fiona Harrison," she said, "do you mind if I ask you a few questions?"

She glanced at Declan, who nodded slightly, then said, "of course."

The detective gestured to the door, and escorted her to an interview room.

"You are..." she looked in her file, "Lily White of White Family Investigations?"

"Yes."

"You are the Granddaughter of Lewis White deceased?"

"Yes."

"You reported a break-in at your offices in the Nicholas Building?"

"Yes."

"And at that time, all that you could say for sure was missing, was the contents of your laptop?"

"Yes."

"You arrived this morning with this thumb drive?" she held up what looked like the thumb drive in a small, sealed plastic bag with a couple of signatures across the seal.

"I can't be sure it's the *same* drive, but it looks like the one I discovered taped underneath my desk this morning, and ran down the street to the station with."

The detective rolled her eyes, then opened up the laptop to reveal one of the photos in the series, "do these photos look familiar?"

"Yes, it looks like one of the ones I discovered on the thumb drive."

"And can you identify either the two main combatants or any of the others in the photograph?"

Lily had only noticed the characters in the foreground, so she leaned forward to look at the men watching along the sidelines.

"Ummm, no, I don't think so."

"What about the location?"

Lily looked again, thinking it might have been the alleyway behind the building, but she didn't recognise it.

"No."

"And do you know what they're doing in this picture?"

She glanced at Declan again before she answered, "illegal street fight? Gang justice? Football rivalry?"

"Can you think of any reason why Mr White might have had this in his possession?"

"Evidence obviously."

"Of what?"

"How would I know? I only know of three ongoing investigations; lost dog in Heidelberg, art theft in Moonee Ponds, and a missing person in Northcote.

"These photos might have been taken for any one of them. Or simply be something he saw while he was out somewhere else.

"If I had his daybook, I could check whether he wrote anything down about them."

The detective opened the file and pulled out a notebook, encased in an evidence bag. "Is this the daybook you're referring to?"

"Yes."

The detective broke the seal and handed it to Lily, who flicked through the pages until she got to the one with the date of the photographs.

"Let's see..."

"What language is that?" asked the detective.

"What? Oh," Lily laughed and marked her place on the page with a finger, "it's Elvish.

Gramps was really taken with *The Lord of the Rings*, and taught himself the runes. Next to no one can read any further than the return address if they find one of the daybooks. We all had to learn.

"Ah, while I think of it, was his camera kit in the car when you found it? There might be more recent evidence in there."

The room went still, "I see. You didn't find the camera."

She went back to the book and kept reading, flipping through a few pages before and after.

"No, nothing about the photos, though he did find the missing artwork and return it, so now I can close that one off and send them their final invoice."

"What about the last few days. Was there anything that made him think hiding the drive was a good idea?"

Lily kept reading, "no mention of it. I wonder if he thought to keep me safe by not writing it down.

"Or was he attempting to blackmail that guy? I can't think why he would do that.

"Maybe he was holding it for someone..."

She flipped back a few pages and started reading again, "could this have been the "artwork" he retrieved?"

She glanced up at the detective, who had a weird look on her face, half incredulity, half pity, "what?"

"Do you know who Leo Palleschi is?"

"No. Should I?"

She tapped the big man in the photo, "this is Leo Palleschi, he's a relatively well-known gang enforcer."

"Ah. I'm beginning to get the picture.

"Did Gramps really die of a heart attack?"

"Yes, it's been confirmed. There are some post-mortem injuries, so perhaps he saw Palleschi coming and died of fright."

"I see.

Lily gulped down the remains of her cold, unpalatable coffee.

"Am I in danger?"

"That rather depends on who wanted the pictures.

"Any chance you could take a vacation?"

"Are you planning to use my office as a trap?"

"We might."

"Do I have any choice?"

"Of course you do, but I imagine you'd like to catch whoever's responsible for your grandfather's death. And to be able to resume your work without fear of reprisals?"

There was no *real* choice.

"Constable Gill can escort you back to the premises to collect your things, then take you home."

«« • »»

It was a little over a week before she was permitted to re-enter the office.

She stood outside the door, wiping her hands down her jeans, afraid of what she might see when she opened the door.

She took a deep breath, closed her eyes, and flung the door open.

It appeared more or less as it had before all this happened. Neat and clean, though she had no idea where all the papers went.

A large bunch of flowers almost engulfed the coffee table, and on the desk was a large stack of mail.

She couldn't face opening the inner door just yet. She knew when she did, she'd see Gramps turning to meet her with his wild white hair and three-piece suit. So she left it shut, and moved to her desk, dumping her bag and the mail on the filing cabinet.

Lily sighed and wondered who would drop Gramps things back, and when.

And then she sighed and thought about all the work closing the office down entailed.

And then there was a tentative knock on the door, so faint she barely heard it.

Lily got up to open it and startled a woman a couple of paces back.

"Can I help you?"

"Is this White Family Investigations?"

"Yes it is, would you like to come in?"

"Oh, I'm not sure... I only... I..."

"Come and sit down, tell me what it is you're worried about?"

"Well, I..."

"At least come in away from prying eyes."

The woman sat on the edge of an armchair; her handbag cradled in her lap. "Well, you see. My boyfriend borrowed some money, and now he's stopped answering his phone, and I'm worried something terrible has happened to him."

And just like that, she was on a new case. There would be plenty of time to take care of the office.

THE END

ABOUT THE AUTHOR

Alexandria Blaelock writes stories, some of them for *Ellery Queen's Mystery Magazine* and *Pulphouse Fiction Magazine*.

She's also written five self-help books applying business techniques to personal matters like getting dressed, cleaning house, and feeding your friends.

She lives in a forest because she enjoys birdsong, and the smell of gum leaves. When not telecommuting to parallel universes from her Melbourne based imagination, she watches K-dramas, talks to animals, and drinks Campari. At the same time.
Discover more at www.alexandriablaelock.com.

IF YOU ENJOYED THIS STORY…

… you might like the other Wilksinson's stories

… the whole collection

... or the first Georgia Garside

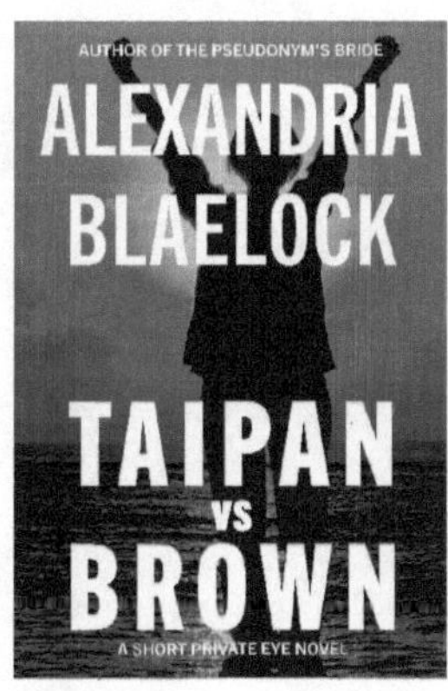

The Robin Hood of Private Investigators

Georgia Garside. Foul-mouthed Private Investigator. Ex-contorionist.

Out of her depth. In over her head.

Caught up in the war between a wealthy industrialist and the ex-sugar babe who can't take a hint.

A laugh-out-loud tripartite battle of wits, winner takes all.